Tins on a Till

Written by Roisin Leahy

Illustrated by Rachel Moss

Collins

red tins
· · ·   · · · ·

big hat
· · · · · ·

red tins

big hat

a till

a fun bag

a till

a fun bag

kick

a mess
· · · —

kick

a mess

14

 Review: After reading

Use your assessment from hearing the children read to choose any GPCs and words that need additional practice.

Read 1: Decoding

- Use grapheme cards to make any words you need to practise. Model reading those words, using teacher-led blending.
- Look at the "I spy sounds" pages (14–15) together. Ask the children to point out as many things as they can in the picture that begin with the /r/ sound. (e.g. *rose, reading, rabbits, raspberries, rain, rice, radio*) Repeat for things that end in "ss". (e.g. *dress, mess, chess*)
- Ask the children to follow as you read the whole book, demonstrating fluency and prosody.

Read 2: Vocabulary

- Look back through the book and discuss the pictures. Encourage the children to talk about details that stand out for them. Use a dialogic talk model to expand on their ideas and recast them in full sentences as naturally as possible.
- Work together to expand vocabulary by naming objects in the pictures that children do not know.
- Turn to page 7. Ask the children: Which word describes the bag? (*fun*) What makes it **fun**? (e.g. *the funny pictures on it*)

Read 3: Comprehension

- Encourage the children to talk about tins. Ask: Have you ever seen tins in a shop, or had them delivered to where you live? What was inside them? What would you like to have that's in a tin?
- Look at pages 6 and 7. Ask: Why do you think there are tins on the till? (e.g. *someone decided not to buy them, they are on display*)
- Turn to pages 10 and 11. Talk about what has happened. Ask: What has gone wrong here? Why do you think this happened? (e.g. *the man accidentally kicked over the display of tins, perhaps because he wasn't looking where he was going*)